LYTTLE LIES

THE STINKY TRUTH

JOE BERGER

SIMON & SCHUSTER

LONDON   NEW YORK   TORONTO   SYDNEY   NEW DELHI

PHEW!

Have you ever felt the weight of the world on your shoulders?

Have you ever wanted, desperately, to be able to turn back the clock, and do something differently – or not do something at all?

If you haven't, you're lucky.

It's the loveliest feeling to have nothing preying on your mind, no dark clouds looming… I felt like that once – for just a few fleeting moments. Three weeks ago, at the beginning of the summer holidays…

PFTT!

THREE
WEEKS
EARLIER

RIIIINNNGGG!

RIIIINNNGGG!

HOORAY! HOORAY!

It's been a stressful year, but my worries have evaporated with the coming of summer.

For a long time, the bane of my life was the school bully,

FEENY.

But since he got made to join the Head Teacher's Gardening Club, everything's changed. I have to hand it to the Head – it seems like his bizarre discipline technique actually has its merits; at least where Feeny's concerned. Feeny's gone from being a cheeseburger-munching school menace to a mild-mannered, salad-loving vegetarian.

FEENY THEN ➡ FEENY NOW

He's also had his hell-hound Butcher re-homed, since he no longer believes dogs should be kept in the city. The only downside to all this is Feeny's show-and-tells, which are now looooong booooring lectures on sustainability (whatever that is) and vegan recipes.

So school is over for another year. And another, even MORE marvellous thing has happened. Drumroll, please…

We're **not** going on a summer holiday!!

Okay, so you're probably thinking that sounds like a bad thing, and I suppose it might be, under normal circumstances, but … double drumroll, please – Charlie's not going away either!!! Which means we get to spend the whole summer, every single hot, dusty never-ending second of it, doing 'that thing', what's it called? That important thing children need to do? Oh, yes, that's right – NOTHING! Kicking about to our hearts' content.

It gets even better…

In three weeks' time it's the neighbourhood carnival.

NEIGHBOURHOOD CARNIVAL!
FLOATS!
MUSIC!
STALLS!
FANCY DRESS PARADE!
OPEN-AIR CINEMA SCREENING!

Everyone is going to be involved, even my mum (though she doesn't know it yet (ahem)). It's going to be super-fun – and the absolute best thing about it is … TRIPLE drumroll – an open-air screening of *Cry Wolfe*. Charlie and I are officially the world's biggest fans of the greatest crime-fighter ever:

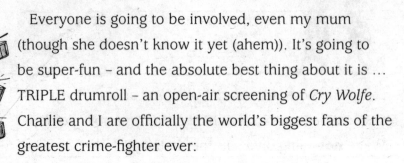

We follow the reruns on TV, but we've never had a chance to see the original made-for-TV, feature-length Wolfe Stone movie. It's super rare, and the chance to see it on the big screen is a once-in-a-lifetime opportunity.

Who knew we weren't the only Wolfe Stone fans in the neighbourhood?

Technically, the holidays start tomorrow. And the moment they start; well, they've begun to end, haven't they? That's why the last day of school is so special. It's limbo time, and I love every second of it. Of which there are approximately two hundred, before I walk through the front door, back to a reality splashdown…

My dad spends ninety-nine per cent of his free time practising his jazz-guitar noodling. Mum doesn't love jazz-guitar noodling roughly one hundred and ten per cent of the time. So he's been banished to the allotment. I think his feelings are a bit hurt, but he's putting a brave face on it. And Grandpa doesn't seem to share Mum's jazz allergy.

I BELIEVE THIS IS WHAT'S KNOWN AS A 'LETTER' — ITS USE HAS SIGNIFICANTLY DECREASED SINCE THE ADVENT OF ELECTRONIC MAIL, MOBILE-MESSAGING ETC. BUT IT WAS ONCE THE PRIMARY FORM OF INDIRECT PERSON-TO-PERSON COMMUNICATION. NOWADAYS IT'S MOSTLY USED AS A PLOT DEVICE IN NOVELS AND OTHER WORKS OF FICTION, YOU KNOW? SORT OF SETTING IN MOTION A CHAIN OF EVENTS THAT LEADS...

AND WHAT'S WRITTEN ON THIS PARTICULAR LETTER, SAM?

..LOOKS LIKE ..WORDS?

HERE, LET ME HELP. IT'S FROM THE CARNIVAL COMMITTEE.

SWIPE!

BLINK BLINK

Dear Mrs Lyttle,
It is with great pleasure we contact you today.
You have been chosen to lead a "charity Zumbathon" in this year's Neighbourhood Carnival. Your "Olympic-standard Zumba dancing" is bound to get everybody moving, and ensure the day is a huge success.

WOW! I HAD NO IDEA YOU WERE AN OLYMPIC ZUMBA DANCER.

I DON'T EVEN KNOW WHAT ZUMBA DANCING IS!

THAT MAKES TWO OF US.

THING IS, THEY CAME TO SCHOOL TO TALK TO US ABOUT THE CARNIVAL. DYLAN TOLD THEM HIS DAD CAN BLOW FIREBALLS WHILE PLAYING THE FLUTE.

DAISY SAID HER MUM WAS A TRAPEZE ARTIST. I JUST DIDN'T WANT YOU TO BE LEFT OUT.

SO YOU LIED!

WELL, NOT TECHNICALLY LYING, BECAUSE YOU ARE GOOD AT DANCING! AND YOU LOVE A CHALLENGE!

AND YOU LIED AGAIN, JUST NOW, WHEN I ASKED YOU ABOUT IT.

LET'S NOT GET OVEREXCITED HERE.

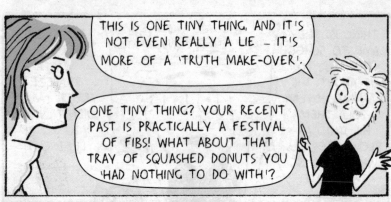

THIS IS ONE TINY THING, AND IT'S NOT EVEN REALLY A LIE — IT'S MORE OF A 'TRUTH MAKE-OVER'.

ONE TINY THING? YOUR RECENT PAST IS PRACTICALLY A FESTIVAL OF FIBS! WHAT ABOUT THAT TRAY OF SQUASHED DONUTS YOU 'HAD NOTHING TO DO WITH'?

THAT WASN'T ACTUALLY ME! IT WAS MY **BUM!**

CAN I HELP IT IF MY BUM HEARS SOME MUSIC AND STARTS DANCING ME ALL AROUND THE KITCHEN?

UP ON TO A CHAIR AND THEN THE WORK-SURFACE?

AND THEN LANDS ME SMACK-BANG IN THE MIDDLE OF A TRAY OF DONUTS?

WE ARE NOT REVISITING THAT CONVERSATION.

AND JUST LAST WEEK YOU TOLD US YOU'D WON THE SCHOOL SPELLING BEE!

THAT WAS TOTALLY AN ALTERNATIVE FACT, BECAUSE I ABSOLUTELY WOULD HAVE WON IF IT HADN'T BEEN CANCELLED BECAUSE THE DEPUTY HEAD GOT MAULED BY AN ESCAPED TREE FROG!

GOSH, HOW AWFUL...

MUM...

OH, SAM!

I JUST DON'T KNOW WHAT TO DO TO GET YOU TO STOP THE INCESSANT FIBBING!

Hear that? That's my 'Suzy Sense'.
It goes off when my big sis is on to me.
She (allegedly) only has my best interests at heart – but she has a killer instinct for how to hit me where it really, really hurts.

HE AND CHARLIE CAN'T WAIT FOR THIS 'ONCE IN A (SAD PERSON'S) LIFETIME EXPERIENCE' - THEY'VE BEEN GOING ON ABOUT IT FOR MONTHS.

NO, NO!

AND NOW IT'S JUST THREE WEEKS AWAY.

NO, NO, NO! YOU CAN'T MAKE ME MISS THE SCREENING - THAT'S NOT FAIR! WE'RE NOT EVEN GETTING A PROPER SUMMER HOLIDAY.

I KNOW I SAID THAT WAS A BONUS EARLIER - BUT IT'S GUILT-TRIP GOLD.

ALL RIGHT. THANK YOU, SUZY.

HERE'S THE DEAL, SAM.

Something is lurking there – something I've dumped in the deepest bargain bin of my mind … a faint shadow…

It never seems to occur to anyone that whistles can get grubby. . .

SO DO YOU, SAM LYTTLE, FORMALLY ACCEPT THE TRUTH CHALLENGE?

YOU CAN DO IT, SAM.

ALL RIGHT! I ACCEPT!

BRING ON THE TRUTH!

That's my big sister Suzy, always looking out for me.
Apparently.

Here's the thing. I don't lie out of some sort of principle. I'm not, like, a warrior monk of lying, wandering the world telling fibs.

Me, I'm more of a panic-liar. Accidents happen, and I don't want to get into trouble, so I have to 'think on my feet'.

Which is hard when your feet are busy running away as fast as they can.

But all that has to change. No more running away.

Staying on the 'straight and narrow' might sound easy enough – but in fact the path of truth is a treacherous health and safety nightmare.

Every way you turn, there are gloopy, eggy bogs,

and gassy sinkholes that could do you in.

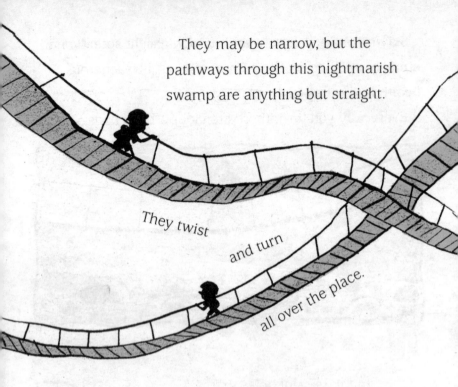

They may be narrow, but the pathways through this nightmarish swamp are anything but straight.

They twist

and turn

all over the place.

There are slats missing ...

… and you never know when you might hit a dead end, and have to backtrack or improvise.

Am I prepared? Let's see…

I have no compass, or torch, or noseplugs.

I forgot to bring a waterproof jacket in case it rains.

At least I have lollies…

But I do know where I need to get to. Somewhere on the other side of this swamp, in three weeks' time, is a glorious fun-filled carnival, and an open-air movie-screening of the coolest crime-fighter the world has ever seen. And all I need to do is rise to the challenge before me, and stick to the truth.

TIME REMAINING TILL CARNIVAL

1 8 0 6 1 7

DAYS　　　HOURS　　　MINUTES

WHAT'S MORE IMPORTANT?

HOW DO YOU CHOOSE BETWEEN JUSTICE ...

AND LOYALTY?

THIS GUY'S BEEN PULLING BANK JOBS ALL DOWN THE WEST COAST; HE'S ALWAYS ONE STEP AHEAD OF US.

AS LONG AS YOU GET THROUGH THE TRUTH CHALLENGE. HOW'S THAT GOING, BY THE WAY?

I DON'T KNOW WHAT ALL THE FUSS IS ABOUT — IT'S ALREADY DAY THREE, AND IT TURNS OUT TELLING THE TRUTH IS EASY-PEASY. FRANKLY, I'M A TEENY BIT INSULTED THAT THEY THINK I WON'T BE ABLE TO DO IT. DO THEY NOT REALIZE WHO I AM?

I THINK THEY PROBABLY DO, UNFORTUNATELY.

SAM, THE PUPIL VOTED 'MOST LIKELY TO BECOME A HEADLINE ON THE EVENING NEWS'.

OKAY, THAT IS TRUE – BUT I DON'T THINK IT WAS MEANT IN A GOOD WAY.

THESE PEOPLE, CHARLIE – THEY MISPRIZE MY GUMPTION.

THERE ARE AT LEAST TWO WORDS IN THAT SENTENCE I DON'T UNDERSTAND.

IN ANY CASE, IF YOU RUN INTO TROUBLE WITH THE CHALLENGE, YOU NEVER KNOW; MAYBE ALIENS WILL FINALLY ARRIVE ON EARTH AT SOME POINT DURING THE NEXT THREE WEEKS.

HOW WOULD THAT HELP?

DON'T YOU EVER THINK ABOUT HOW THAT WOULD JUST CHANGE EVERYTHING? NOTHING WE THINK MATTERS WOULD MATTER ANY MORE. BECAUSE — ALIENS! ACTUAL LIFE FORMS FROM ANOTHER ACTUAL PLANET. LIKE, MY MUM WOULD BE IN THE MIDDLE OF TELLING ME OFF FOR NOT LOADING THE DISHWASHER, AND SUDDENLY ... 'SORRY, CHARLIE, NEVER MIND — ACTUAL ALIENS!'

BUT THEY MIGHT NOT BE FRIENDLY.

EVEN LESS REASON TO WORRY ABOUT WHETHER I'VE LOADED THE DISHWASHER. IT'S A WIN-WIN.

RIIIGHT.

WELL, I THINK I'D BETTER TRY AND STICK TO THE CHALLENGE FOR NOW — YOU KNOW, IN THE UNLIKELY EVENT THAT THE ALIENS ARE RUNNING A DAY OR SO LATE.

I'LL DO EVERYTHING I CAN TO HELP YOU, SAM — AFTER ALL, IT'S CRY WOLFE THAT'S AT STAKE HERE. WE WILL NEVER GET ANOTHER CHANCE TO SEE THE GREAT STRAIGHT-TO-VIDEO, BARGAIN-BIN LOST MASTERPIECE ON THE BIG SCREEN EVER AGAIN!

DON'T WORRY, CHARLIE — I'VE GOT THIS.

Speaking of challenges. Dinner at home has become a bit challenging in itself, since Dad moved his jazz-guitar set-up down to Grandpa's allotment.

If you know my grandpa, you'll know how obsessed he is with radishes.

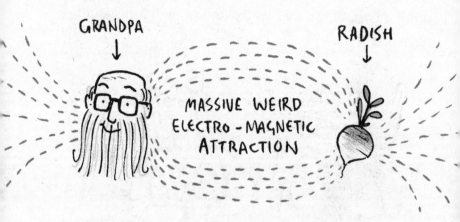

GRANDPA

RADISH

MASSIVE WEIRD
ELECTRO - MAGNETIC
ATTRACTION

Well, I'm afraid the obsession has worsened. As if raw radishes with cold butter and a pinch of salt weren't bad enough (Bleurgh!), now he also PICKLES the radishes!

PICKLED RADISHES!

PICKLED!?

RADISHES!?

One of the peculiar things about the neighbourhood carnival is how many pickle stalls there are – you'd think 'none' would be the ideal number, but instead we have two.

Muriel next door always runs a pickle stall, and so does Grandpa. But every year, Muriel's pickles sell out, while Grandpa has a lot of leftovers. He's determined to sell out this year; it's kind of a pride thing. I think Grandpa's secretly sweet on Muriel, and believes she could never love a man who can't sell his own pickles.

You should see his shed on the allotment. It's lined with shelves and shelves of horrifying pickling experiments.

Imagine if, one night, a plucky ragtag band of radishes hauled themselves out of the ground and went looking for their comrades.

They'd creep under the door...

Flip on the light...

The scene that would greet them would be like something from a horror movie.

Thing is, Grandpa's also a self-taught magician, known as '**THE GREAT WONDEROSO**'.

He taught himself how to disappear a parking ticket (no one's ever found it), and how to turn an orange purple (if you ever see a purple orange, don't eat it). And he taught himself the art of hypnosis – he claims to have successfully hypnotized the slugs on his allotment to despise radishes. Maybe they're hypnotized, maybe they're just sensible? Anyway, the point is, he doesn't like to learn from books. He says:

YOU WON'T FIND ANSWERS IN BOOKS, SAM, ONLY QUESTIONS.

He takes this same 'no-instruction-manuals' approach with pickling – but you can't learn a lot from talking to a jar of pickled radishes. You have to use something called 'trial and error'. And that is, I'm afraid, what makes dinner so challenging. The 'error' can be quite serious when all sorts of vile herbs, spices and sweet and sour liquids are involved, and the 'trial' part involves putting these things in your poor, unsuspecting mouth.

Oh, yes, there's something I forgot to mention. Grandpa's convinced that the secret to the elusive magical pickling formula is Dad's jazz-guitar noodling.

Since Dad moved his sound system down to the allotment, the vegetables are growing bigger and faster and, apparently, tastier than ever before. Each batch of pickles is named after the tune that Dad was jamming whilst Grandpa tossed random stinky nasties into the pickling vat.

MMM, SEE IF YOU CAN TASTE THE JAZZ.

GOSH, THEY'RE REALLY ... UNUSUAL...

VERY ... UM, FLAVOURSOME.

SAM? WHAT DO YOU THINK, BOYO?

THE THING IS, I'M NOT SUPPOSED TO LIE...

EVEN A LITTLE BIT...

BUT I THINK THEY'RE...

YES?!

THE WORD I WANT TO USE IS...

THERE'S A SORT OF ... EGGY UNDERCURRENT.

HMM, THAT MIGHT BE THE FUNKY BASS BACKING TRACK — MY FAULT ENTIRELY.

ALMOST A ... CHEESINESS.

I THINK I WENT OVERBOARD WITH THE WAH WAH PEDAL.

SCRIBBLE

AND JUST THE FAINTEST WHIFF OF A, ALMOST A ... STINKY SWAMP PONG.

I DON'T THINK THAT'S ME.

BUT YOU ALL DISAGREE? YOU LIKED THEM?

WELL, SAM MIGHT HAVE A POINT.

THEY MIGHT NOT BE QUITE THERE YET, GRANDPA...

This is true – Dad's taste buds were zapped in a bizarre accident involving a faulty guitar amp and a lightning storm in the late 1990s. Which does make me question his usefulness as a pickling partner – no one else seems to be bothered, though.

ANY TIME.

YOU KNOW, SOME OF THE BEST JAZZ TUNES TOOK YEARS TO PERFECT. YOU CAN'T RUSH ART.

So I'm off and running …

… let's just hope this **STINKY SWAMP OF TRUTH** doesn't have too many creepy surprises in it.

If I'm honest …

… this 'telling the truth' lark is actually pretty straightforward once you get into the swing of it.

WOULD YOU LIKE TO HELP ME WITH THE SHOPPING, SAM?

NOPE!

SAM!

I WILL HELP YOU, BUT I WOULDN'T 'LIKE TO', WHICH IS WHAT YOU ASKED. IT'S THE TRUTH, SEE?

HEY, SIS.

I THINK THAT NAIL VARNISH IS A BIT HEAVY, SUZY. FOR THIS TIME OF DAY YOU MIGHT WANT TO TRY SOMETHING A LITTLE BIT LESS ... I DON'T KNOW...

WHO ASKED YOU, SAM? OH, THAT'S RIGHT — NO ONE!

WELL, I JUST FEEL IT'S GOOD PRACTICE TO BE AS HONEST AS POSSIBLE — I'M GOING FOR 'FULL TRANSPARENCY'.

MUUUM! SAM'S 'TRUTHING' AGAIN.

I KNOW, I KNOW. IT WON'T LAST FOREVER, SUZY — JUST TRY TO ZONE IT OUT.

TIME REMAINING TILL CARNIVAL

0 9 0 2 2 2

DAYS   HOURS   MINUTES

Telling the truth may be easy, but staying out of trouble can be harder – especially when you've got so much 'nothing' to do.

I know, I know, I said I was really looking forward to doing nothing all summer – but that's only fun when it happens together with Charlie. And when he's not around because he's got to buy shoes or go to a silly wedding or whatever – time really starts to drag. And that's when accidents happen.

For instance, who could have foreseen that a simple piece of plastic tubing would create untold havoc?

Not me.

All I did was pick it up and whoosh it round my head a couple of times, and discover that it made a marvellous low, droning whooshy sound.

LOW DRONING WHOOSHY WHOOSH...

(Well, actually I did know this would happen, I have tried it once before.)

And how was I supposed to know that doing this in the sitting room would be a BIG mistake?

(Again, now that I think about it,
that is what I did last time.)

But honestly – who would leave
that stupid clock on the side table
AGAIN where it could get knocked off
on to the floor AGAIN and the glass
face broken AGAIN?

Okay, the last time this happened I put the clock back on the table and ran away. When it was discovered I denied any involvement. Which was 'lying'. So this time, when the exact same thing happens, I have a careful think.

I go to Mum, and explain what happened. Mum is very cross, and I will have to pay for the damage to the clock from my pocket money. But I have told the truth! I stayed on the right path.

TIME REMAINING TILL CARNIVAL

DAYS   HOURS   MINUTES

Meanwhile, everyone else is so busy that they keep out of my way.

Grandpa and Dad are rattling through many further iterations of pickle disaster,

but success so far continues
to elude them.

Mum is rising to the Zumba challenge.

She's co-opted several of my friends' mums (including

Charlie's) to join the Zumba Mums charity Zumbathon.

It is a little more ambitious than I had in mind when I mentioned it to the committee.

My friends are not thrilled about this.

I GUESS IF IT MAKES THEM HAPPY...

Even Suzy's got the carnival bug. She's running a stall selling all her old toys – it's almost like she *wants* to grow up or something. Weirdo.

She's canvassing the neighbourhood for old toys and games to sell on her charity stall – I imagine the spiel goes something like this:

JOIN ME!

BANISH ALL TRACES OF FUN FROM YOUR HOME!

CAST OFF YOUR CHILDISH WAYS AND PLAY NO MORE!

GROW!

Pudding, on the other hand, is not faring quite so well.

PFFT!

She has begun to produce the most heinous noxious gases, and her fur seems to be getting visibly lighter.

Mum takes her to the vet but she gets a clean bill of health.

I've even had to ban her from the den, which is where Charlie and I go to watch more excerpts from *Cry Wolfe*…

The Following Preview Has Been
Approved for All Audiences

Contains mild peril,
threat of acting and
frequent bad hair

WELL, BACK THEN SHE WAS JUST SWEET MOLLY.

BILLY NEVER FORGAVE ME FOR 'STEALING HER HEART'.

WOLFE STONE?

YOU'RE UNDER ARREST FOR CONSPIRACY TO A CAMPAIGN OF GRAND LARCENY.

BILLY'S TRYING TO FRAME ME FOR THESE BANK JOBS. CHIEF, YOU GOTTA GIVE ME TIME TO FIND HIM AND BRING HIM IN.

TIME REMAINING TILL CARNIVAL

0 3 1 6 0 6

DAYS HOURS MINUTES

The days are ticking by, but my troubled relationship
with the truth continues to be put to the test. Even when
Charlie is around, problems can still occur.

For instance…

Mr EG (our name for
him) is the old man who
lives in the green house
at the top of the road.

It's not an actual greenhouse – in fact it's not even green any more, it's pale orange. But when it was green we called it 'the green house' – 'the pale orange house' doesn't sound right so we still call it the green house … we know what we mean.

We have long suspected him of being an Evil Genius (which is what EG stands for), so when we see him taking delivery of a sinister-shaped box …

… it's pretty obvious that it will contain components for a giant death ray.

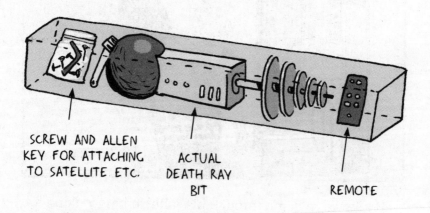

SCREW AND ALLEN KEY FOR ATTACHING TO SATELLITE ETC.

ACTUAL DEATH RAY BIT

REMOTE

All the signs are there:

SIGN 1:

The box says,

AUDIO/VISUAL PROJECTOR SCREEN

on the side, which is EXACTLY what you'd write on it if you didn't want people to know it was components for a giant death ray.

SIGN 2:

While we're going through his rubbish bins looking for evidence of evil plans, he jumps out on us and chases us away.

What's he trying to hide?

SIGN 3:

He somehow (spy satellite? network of informants (including my sister, perhaps)?) knows where I live, and comes to speak to my mum.

SIGN 4:

He is irrationally angry and upset about the mess we've made, another clear sign that he is up to no good.

My mum calls me and Charlie …

… we are hiding in a shoe chest at this point, listening in on the conversation to see if we have enough evidence to warn the government.

That's when Mum spots us. It's embarassing. It's awkward.

The old me would have tried to lie my way out.

I SWEAR — WE ONLY WENT IN HIS BIN BECAUSE WE SAW A LEPRECHAUN HIDING IN IT, AND I JUST WANTED TO RETURN THE POT OF GOLD TO ITS RIGHTFUL OWNER...

The new me, the one who desperately wants to win the challenge, apologizes.

SORRY.

My mum is, again, fairly grumpy about the whole thing, but I did tell the truth. In any case, she's got more important things to do, like work out how to Zumba dance for three hours straight, in a week's time.

I'm pretty proud of her actually – she's really going for it with the Zumba. She's so excited about it she's keeping a calendar where she marks off the days to the big event. At least I think that's what it's about.

So onwards I plod through the bog, keeping my head down and my eyes on the prize.

And almost before you can say

IT WASN'T ME I DIDN'T DO IT WHY DOESN'T ANYONE EVER BELIEVE ME IT'S TRUE I TELL YOU!

it's the eve of the big day itself.

TIME REMAINING TILL CARNIVAL

0 0 2 0 5 4

DAYS   HOURS   MINUTES

I've nearly done it. I've navigated a tricky path through the stinky swamp of truth; the mists are clearing, the bogs are drying out, and success is within sight.

Which is, of course, when it all goes horribly wrong.

SAM – A WORD, PLEASE.

OKAY.

FLOCCINAUCINIHILIPILIFICATION!

SIGH.

IT MEANS...

YES ... THE ABSOLUTE ESTIMATED WORTHLESSNESS, AND IT'S THE SECOND-LONGEST WORD IN THE ENGLISH LANGUAGE; YOU'VE DONE THIS ONE BEFORE.

So Charlie and I go to pick up the parcel, little suspecting the disaster that awaits…

BILLY IS A GHOST, CHIEF. A GHOST FROM THE PAST.

YOU WON'T GET AWAY WITH THIS, BILLY — DON'T BE A FOOL.

HEY, SAM, I'VE JUST HAD A GREAT IDEA. TOMORROW AT THE CARNIVAL, WE COULD DRESS UP AS WOLFE STONE AND BAD TIMIN' BILLY!

On the reverse of this mystery parcel is the return address – a holiday cottage we stayed at ages ago.

When I see it, a tiny alarm bell goes off in my head.

OPEN IT A BIT MORE. HERE. LET ME HELP.

WRENCH...

POP!

OOPS!

OKAY, WELL THAT'S THAT THEN.

'THAT' IS THE END OF THE ROAD, CHARLIE! 'THAT' SPELLS DISASTER FOR THE TRUTH CHALLENGE, AND MY HOPES OF SEEING CRY WOLFE ON THE BIG SCREEN.

HEY, LOOK, HERE COMES YOUR SISTER.

GAH!

CHARLIE, CAN WE GO TO YOUR HOUSE?

YOU BET.

STUFF!

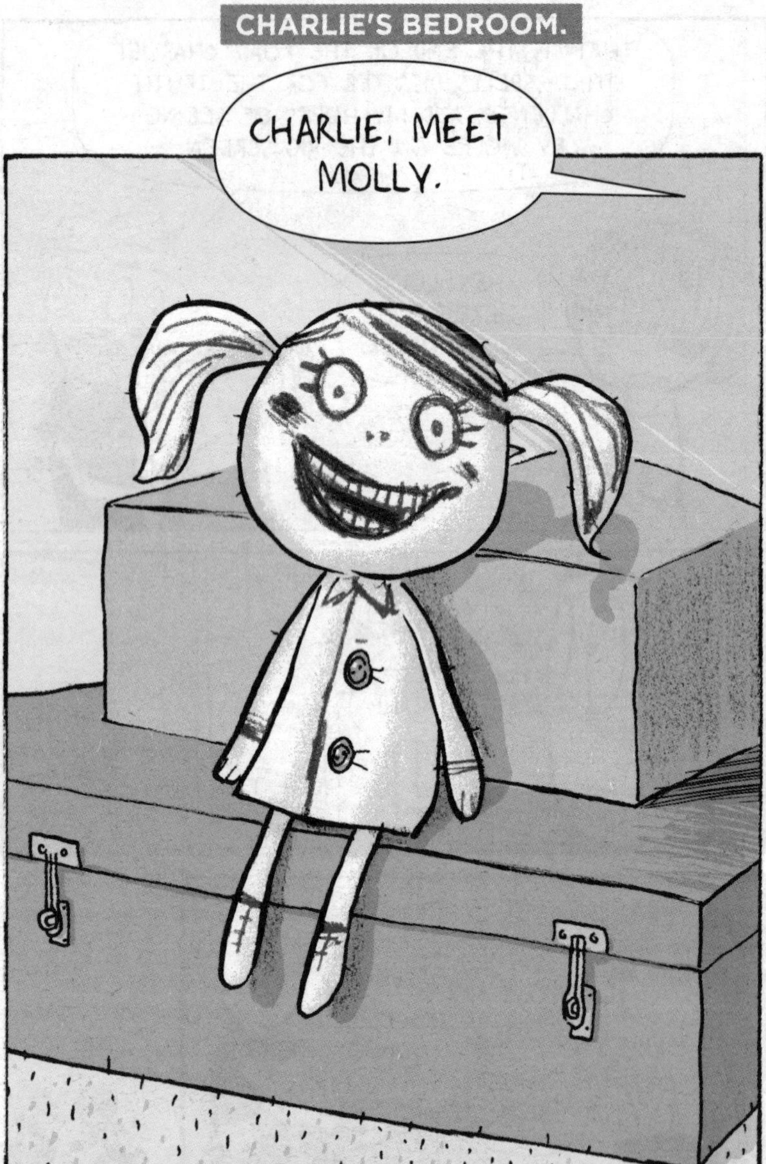
CHARLIE'S BEDROOM.
CHARLIE, MEET MOLLY.

WE'RE ON A FAMILY SUMMER HOLIDAY
IN A COTTAGE BY THE SEA.

SUZY'S BROUGHT HER BELOVED
CLOTHKIT DOLL, MOLLY.

SHE ADORES THIS DOLL, EVEN THOUGH IT'S JUST STITCHED OUT OF PLAIN FABRIC — NO DETAIL AT ALL, NOT EVEN A FACE. NOT EVEN ANY EYES!

OH, SORRY, CHARLIE.

I HAVE EYES; I JUST CHOOSE TO KEEP THEM TO MYSELF.

I'VE BROUGHT A STACK OF SUPERHERO COMICS. I DON'T REALLY READ THEM, BUT I LIKE LOOKING AT THE PICTURES — I'M SECRETLY IN LOVE WITH SHE-HULK (WHO I CALL "SHE'S HULK").

THE SAVAGE SHE-HULK

TOO MUCH TRUTH!

ANYWAY, ON THE LAST DAY OF THE HOLIDAYS, I'M DRAWING AT THE TABLE, WITH MY FAVOURITE PEN, GIVEN TO ME BY GRANDPA.

WHAT LOVELY DRAWINGS, SAM. BE CAREFUL WITH THAT MARKER PEN, THOUGH, IT'S PERMANENT, REMEMBER – DON'T GET ANY ON THE TABLE.

WHY YOUR GRANDPA THOUGHT THAT WAS A SUITABLE PEN FOR A CHILD IS A MYSTERY.

MUM AND SUZY GO OFF TO THE BEACH, AND DAD'S PLAYING JAZZ GUITAR. AND MOLLY'S LOOKING AT ME.

ONLY SHE'S NOT, BECAUSE SHE HAS NO FACE.

AND I SUDDENLY HAVE A BRILLIANT IDEA.

I CAN DRAW PRETTY FACE FOR MOLLY...

PRETTY FACE, LIKE SHE'S HULK.

IT'S POSSIBLE I HAVE AN INFLATED
SENSE OF MY ARTISTIC ABILITY ...

I'M NOT TOTALLY HAPPY WITH THE SMILE —
SO I HAVE ANOTHER GO AT THE MOUTH ...

THEN THE EYES SEEM A BIT PENSIVE, SO I ADD
A BIT MORE LIFE TO THEM, AND THE CHEEKS ...

AND THEN I THINK MAYBE THE FACE IS NOW A LITTLE OUT OF KEEPING WITH THE REST OF THE DOLL, SO I ADD A BIT OF DETAIL TO MAKE IT ALL FIT...

Sam Lyttle

All artistic commissions undertaken

No job too ambitious!

I WAS YOUNG — I DIDN'T UNDERSTAND THAT IT'S BEST TO GET THE ARTISTIC COMMISSION *BEFORE* YOU EMBARK ON THE WORK.

IN FAIRNESS, THE EXACT SAME THING HAPPENED TO MICHELANGELO WITH THE SISTINE CHAPEL CEILING. HE DID THE WHOLE THING AS A SURPRISE FOR POPE JULIUS II — HE HAD TO KEEP HIM FROM COMING INTO THE CHAPEL FOR FOUR YEARS*...

YEAH, WELL, MICHELANGELO, Y'KNOW? PRETTY WELL REGARDED IN THE OLD PERMANENT MARKER DEPARTMENT. YOUNG SAM LYTTLE? NOT SO MUCH.

* this may not be true.

SO WHAT DID YOU DO?

WHAT ELSE COULD I DO? I MEAN, APART FROM CONFESSING.

145

Over time, Suzy forgot about Molly, and no one ever suspected I had anything to do with the disappearance – I gradually buried the awful thing I did in the deepest recesses of my mind. And now, like a ghost from the past, Molly has found her way home.

SAM. WE'VE GOT SOMETHING TO SAY.

WHAT!? IF IT'S ABOUT THE...

JUST A LITTLE SOMETHING TO SAY 'WELL DONE' FOR COMPLETING THE TRUTH CHALLENGE.

CONGRATULATIONS, SAM – YOU MANAGED TO STAY HONEST FOR THE ENTIRE THREE WEEKS.

I'M PROUD OF YOU, SAMMY. YOU'VE CERTAINLY EARNED THIS.

GOOD LAD.

OOH, SAM — DID YOU PICK UP THAT PARCEL FROM THE POST OFFICE FOR ME?

I DID. BUT I LEFT IT AT CHARLIE'S, SORRY. I'LL PICK IT UP AFTER THE CARNIVAL TOMORROW.

POKE...

AH, OKAY.

EESH.

NOW, THEN. MAY I PRESENT TO YOU ALL THE CROWNING GLORY OF PICKLEDOM. I KNOW WE'VE SAID IT BEFORE, BUT THIS TIME I DO BELIEVE WE HAVE CRACKED IT — THE GOLDEN SAMBA PICKLED RADISHES.

OH, BOY, HERE WE GO AGAIN.

WOWEE - FRESH!

TASTY!

You know that bit in adverts on TV, when the person takes a bite of food they're not expecting to be nice and it actually is. They pull a certain kind of face, like:

162

TINGLY...

ZINGY...

SPEAKING AS SOMEONE WHO DOESN'T ACTUALLY LIKE PICKLES, I'VE GOT TO SAY — THESE ARE GOOD.

HIGH PRAISE INDEED!

I KNEW IT! ZUMBA RHYTHMS!

SNAP!

WHAT DID YOU SAY? ZUMBA?

GREAT — CONSIDER YOURSELF BOOKED. THE ZUMBA MUMS JUST GOT LIVE ACCOMPANIMENT!

AND HERE'S TO SAM — FOR GALLANTLY MANAGING TO STICK TO THE TRUTH FOR THREE WHOLE WEEKS! HOWEVER PAINFUL IT PROVED FOR THE REST OF US.

PERHAPS YOU'VE TURNED A CORNER FOR GOOD, SAM!

HEH-HEH, WELL ... I DON'T KNOW ABOUT THAT. WHAT IS TRUTH ANYWAY? IT'S ALL SO ... SUBJECTIVE.

RIGHT. ANY MORE FOR ANY MORE?

CAN I BE EXCUSED? I NEED TO SORT STUFF FOR THE STALL TOMORROW. GRANDPA, CAN I TAKE A PICKLE WITH ME?

BUT OF COURSE!

I'M DONE TOO, THANK YOU.

OH, SAM! WITH ALL THE EXCITEMENT OF THE CARNIVAL TOMORROW, DON'T FORGET...

PARCEL!

RIGHT, PARCEL.

PFFT!

STONE TO BAD-TIMIN' BILLY. COME IN, BTB.

OVER.

... FSSSSSS ...

HOW'S IT GOING, SIS?

ALMOST THERE.

I'VE GOT A LOT OF STUFF, AND THERE'S STILL MORE TO BE DROPPED AT THE STALL TOMORROW.

AREN'T YOU... AREN'T YOU SAD TO BE SEEING THE LAST OF THESE TOYS?

NAH. NONE OF IT MEANS ANYTHING TO ME, NOT REALLY.

THERE WAS ONE DOLL I LOVED BUT ...

I LOST HER.

DON'T LOOK AT ME LIKE THAT.

...CRACKLE...
...FSSST...

You're probably thinking, 'What's the big deal? You've won the challenge. You've even got a shiny new bike.' But it's impossible to enjoy this stuff when there's something weighing on your conscience.

Just impossible.

CLICK!

DRAWN ON
STUBBLE

WOLFE STONE TO BAD TIMIN' BILLY. COME IN, BTB — OVER.

ROGER THAT, STONE. WITH YOU IN A TICK — OVER.

BRING THE GOODS. OVER AND OUT.

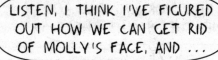

SCREEEECH!

LET'S GO AND ASK NOW. COME ON!

SKID...

SCREEEECH!

HEY, WOLFE AND BILLY – NICE COSTUMES!

☆SUZY'S TOYS & GAMES☆

SAM!

SAM, I THINK I KNOW WHAT HAPPENED TO THE DOLL — AND IT'S BAD.

MY MUM MUST HAVE SCOOPED UP THE BOX WITH SOME OLD TOYS AND STUFF FOR YOUR SISTER — THE BOX IS AT *YOUR SISTER'S STALL!*

WHAAAT! WE HAVE TO GET OVER THERE NOW!

AND A SPECIAL PRIZE FOR 'THEMATIC RELEVANCE' GOES TO ...

WOLFE STONE AND BAD TIMIN' BILLY! FROM MY FAVOURITE TV SHOW! COME ON UP HERE BOYS!

COME ON CHARLIE...

WE'VE GOT TO GET MOLLY!

THANK YOU! SORRY - THIS IS NOT FANCY DRESS - WE'RE ON A MISSION.

NOOOOOO!!

THE EXPERIMENTAL PICKLE JUICE DISSOLVES PERMANENT MARKER - BUT MY MUM MUST HAVE FOUND THE JAR AND POURED THE DREGS AWAY!

I'M DOOMED, CHARLIE. THAT'S IT. GAME OVER. I AM UNDONE. GAH!

WAIT A SECOND...

PERHAPS YOUR GRANDPA HAS SOME OF THE EXPERIMENTAL PICKLES AT HIS STALL.

EH ...? OH MY GOSH!

SLIDE...

LET'S GO! GRAB MOLLY!

GRAB!

THE ZUMBATHON WENT BRILLIANTLY — SAM, THANK YOU FOR PUTTING ME UP FOR IT. I FEEL WONDERFUL. AND YOUR DAD'S PLAYING WAS, WELL, IT WAS ACTUALLY ...

INSPIRATIONAL.

AWW...

OOH, IS THAT THE PARCEL YOU PICKED UP!?

NO...! I MEAN YES, BUT...

WAIT...
WHAT'S THIS?
OH, MY
GOSH ...

...IT'S MOLLY!

IT'S
MOLLY!

I CAN'T BELIEVE PUDDING'S PICKLE FARTS COULD HAVE SUCH AN INCREDIBLE EFFECT.

I KNOW!

THEY WERE SO STRONG THEY DISSOLVED MOLLY'S FACE.

YEAH, AND IT WAS HER FARTS THAT TURNED HER FUR AND MURIEL'S FLOWERS WHITE — THEY WERE RIGHT NEXT TO HER FAVOURITE SNOOZING SPOT.

GRANDPA THINKS THAT NOW THAT SHE HAS NO MORE PICKLE JUICE TO DRINK, SHE'LL GO BACK TO NORMAL.

BUT NOW THAT HE AND DAD HAVE WITNESSED THE AMAZING BLEACHING QUALITIES OF HER FARTS, THEY'RE GOING TO TRY TO RESURRECT THE RECIPE. THEY RECKON THE FORMULA FOR A MIRACLE STAIN-REMOVER GAS COULD BE WORTH A FORTUNE. IF THEY CAN STOP IT PONGING...

ANYWAY, MOLLY'S IN MY BEDROOM, AND THAT'S WHERE SHE'S STAYING. BUT I'LL ALWAYS LOVE HER, AND I'M NOT ASHAMED TO SAY IT.

LOLLY?

THANKS.

THAT'S COMING FROM YOUR HALF, CHARLIE.

Well, against the odds, I made it through the **STINKY SWAMP OF TRUTH**. I thought I was just looking forward to a movie, but it turns out I was after something a little bit more precious and hard to get hold of. A sense of contentment, the bliss of not being responsible for causing any bad stuff.

In my experience, moments like this never last long, but I'm going to savour every last second of it…

Until the next inevitable home-grown calamity.

COME ON OUT BILLY,
THE GAME'S OVER.

GET OUT OF HERE, STONE - YOU TAKE ANOTHER STEP AND I'LL BLOW THIS PLACE SKY HIGH.

WE'VE ALL GOT THINGS FROM OUR PAST WE'D RATHER FORGET, BILLY. THING'S WE'D DO DIFFERENTLY, GIVEN THE CHANCE...

IT'S A LITTLE LATE FOR REGRETS, STONE, DON'T YOU THINK? THE DAMAGE IS DONE. IT'S TIME TO PAY THE PIPER.

YOU EVER HEAR OF 'CHICKENS COMING HOME TO ROOST'? WELL LOOK UP, BECAUSE THAT SKY IS FULL OF HENS.